Sally's Submarine

BY JOAN ANDERSON   PHOTOGRAPHED BY GEORGE ANCONA

St. Louis de Montfort Catholic School
Fishers, IN

MORROW JUNIOR BOOKS   NEW YORK

ACKNOWLEDGMENTS

Many, many thanks to our wonderful Sally, played by Michelle Phillip. Her steadfastness during the difficult photo session was tremendous. Thanks also to Barry Homer, the fisherman father, for his boat and equipment; to Geoffrey Borman, a friend and adviser on mermaids and underwater life; to the children of Bardonia Elementary School, who gave us terrific plot ideas; to the Center for Coastal Studies, who supplied the whale shot; to Ken Porter, who transported the submarine from location to location; to Marina Ancona for her help in the layout of the book; and to Isabel Ancona for her photography at the Monterey Aquarium.

Joan Anderson
George Ancona

The photo on pages 28–29 is courtesy of the Center for Coastal Studies, Inc., Provincetown, Massachusetts.

The text type is 15-point Goudy Sans Bold.
Text copyright © 1995 by Joan Anderson
Photographs copyright © 1995 by George Ancona
Printed in Hong Kong by South China Printing Company (1988) Ltd.
1 2 3 4 5 6 7 8 9 10
Library of Congress Cataloging-in-Publication Data
Anderson, Joan.   Sally's submarine/by Joan Anderson; photographed by George Ancona.   p.   cm.
Summary: Sally's homemade submarine takes her out to sea, to the ocean floor, and back home
just as her fisherman father returns to the dock.
ISBN 0-688-12690-1 (trade)—ISBN 0-688-12691-X (library)
[1. Submarines—Fiction.   2. Marine animals—Fiction.   3. Fathers and daughters—Fiction.]   I. Ancona, George, ill.
II. Title.   PZ7.A5367Sal 1995 [E]—dc20 94-16644 CIP AC

For Susannah Kavanaugh,
our Little Mermaid
—J.A.

For little Natalie
—G.A.

SALLY'S SUB

Every day, all summer long, Sally Sanford helps her father load his fishing boat for a day at sea.

Once it is piled high with lobster traps and fishing poles and buckets of bait, he heads off to sea, leaving Sally behind.

Sometimes Sally spends her time mending nets or baiting hooks. Sometimes she goes crabbing or clamming.

Sometimes she just sits by the water and dreams of going off to sea, like her dad.

What she likes to do best is to climb inside her homemade submarine, close the hatch, and imagine she is diving to the bottom of the ocean. There she wiggles her sub in and out of coral caves or chases monster fish through forests of kelp.

One afternoon, as Sally and her submarine were preparing to surface after a trip to the Arctic Ocean, something weird happened. Sally felt herself pitching and rolling.

What's going on? she wondered.

Splash! came the answer. A giant wave hit her sub's hull. Then another and another. Foamy blue water sloshed outside the portholes, and Sally couldn't see out.

"I'd better push up my periscope and find out where I am," she said.

"Can it be?" Sally asked, panicked and excited at the same time. Squinting, she searched the horizon for the dock and saw it was only a speck. "Wow! This time I really *am* out to sea!"

Sally held tight to the rudder with one hand and the propeller stick with the other as she tried to decide whether or not to go back to shore.

Just then a whiskery black face appeared at a porthole. *Arf, arf,* barked a shiny seal, as if it were saying, Follow me.

"Why not?" Sally said, cranking the propeller to see if her sub could actually move.

In seconds she was off, her sub skimming across the water like a high-speed racing boat. "Whee!" Sally shouted. "This sure is *fun!*"

The seal zigzagged through an obstacle course of buoys, and Sally kept pace with this speedy game of tag. Then the seal dove underwater.

"Aha," Sally said. "Now you want me to play hide-and-seek. Well, here I go!"

Sally leaned on the dive shaft, and her sub plunged just below the surface.

"I see you," she said, spotting her friend's flippers. But in seconds the seal was gone again—heading into the depths.

SALLY'S SUB

"If you can do it, so can I," Sally cried as she pressed hard on the shaft to make a complete dive.

Fizzzzzzzzz, whizzzzzzz! Water hissed and gurgled around the little sub as down, down, down Sally sank. She went past giant clumps of seaweed, schools of frightened fish, patches of snowy algae until...*thud.* Sally's submarine came to rest on the ocean floor.

Once the sand settled after the impact, Sally was amazed at what she saw. Looking out a porthole was like gazing into a tropical aquarium. Fish of every color, shape, and size weaved around jutting rocks and in and out of shrubs of sea lettuce.

Before Sally could wonder what to do first, a giant lobster crept out of a crevice and headed straight for the bait inside a nearby lobster trap.

"Hey, don't go in there!" Sally shouted, knowing what would happen to the lobster if it swam into the trap.

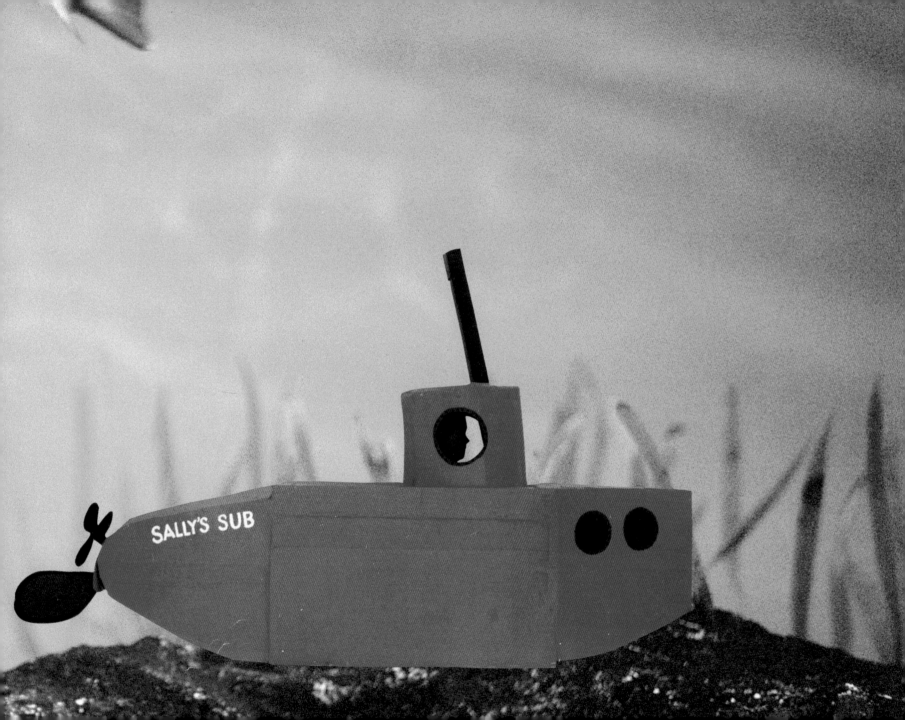

Without even thinking about it, Sally threw open the hatch and swam out into the chilly water. *"Brrrr."* Sally shivered as she glided toward the slow-moving lobster.

"Gotcha!" she said, clutching the lobster's shell and heading it in another direction. "Phew!" she sighed. "Another lobster saved from the pot of boiling water."

Sally sat on the empty trap, gazing around at the bright orange starfish and pink-streaked whelks nestling with giant clams.

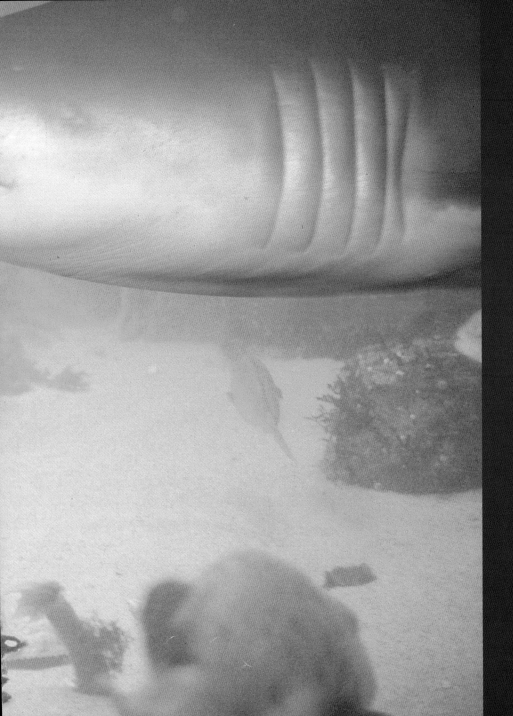

She was just beginning to enjoy this underwater world when she noticed a huge dark shape heading toward her.

Something told Sally to move—quickly. She swam behind the lobster trap and peered over it. "Oh, no!" she gasped, staring at a large-headed fish with a mouth full of razor-sharp teeth. A shark!

Her heart pounded. Where could she hide? What should she do?

Just then the lobster trap jerked... then moved across the sand...then started to rise. "Not now!" Sally wailed, realizing that the fisherman who had set this trap was hauling it in.

Hey, why not go along? Sally thought, and quickly grabbed on.

Up, up, up she went.

The boat kept moving as the fisherman tugged on the line. Sally held tight, riding along through the whirling currents. Suddenly she was at the surface.

"Finally," Sally sighed, spitting out a mouthful of salty water. She felt ready to be rescued! But the fisherman didn't see her. He saw only an empty trap, and he promptly dropped it right back into the sea.

"Ouch!" Sally yelped as her body hit the water. And down she tumbled, back to the bottom.

"Now where am I?" Sally cried, feeling sad and weary for the first time.

Arf, arf was the reply.

"Who's there?" Sally called, floating toward the sound. She didn't have to wonder very long before a sleek black body glided up to her.

"My seal!" Sally squealed. "Where have you been? Can you help me find my submarine?"

The seal flapped its flippers as if to say yes, and Sally followed, matching her friend stroke for stroke. As they swam, curious codfish nibbled at Sally's fingernails, while angelfish tugged at her hair and tickled her scalp.

"I hope you're leading me somewhere," Sally said. Her arms were tired and she wanted to rest. Then she saw a splotch of orange up ahead.

"Hurray!" Sally gurgled as she swam closer to the mound of sand on which her submarine lay waiting. A few more strokes and she reached the hatch. With another swift movement she pulled it open and squirmed inside.

"Phew!" she said, relieved to be back in her sub. But just then the water outside the portholes turned from a pretty blue to a dark gray, as if a giant cloud had moved in.

"Now what? I'd better get out of here," Sally said as she cranked the propeller to move her sub—fast.

She pressed on the surfacing shaft, and the little submarine groaned into action. With one big swish they were moving. The portholes gleamed with bubbles until suddenly—*pop! splash!*—Sally and her sub shot up like the top exploding off a teakettle, and she found that she had surfaced right next to a big glob of land. Or was it a sandbar? Or maybe an island?

But then the island snorted and squealed and gave a long, deep whoop as it leaped out of the water.

"That's no island!" yelped Sally. "That's a whale!"

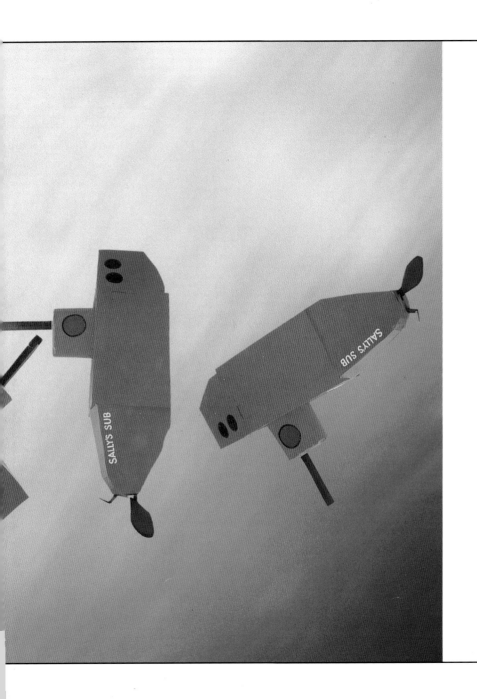

Before she could maneuver out of its way, the whale dove, flipping its enormous tail—and creating a current that sent Sally's submarine rolling, shaking, and twirling toward land.

Thump! The little sub came to a halt right up on the shore. Sally popped open the hatch just as her dad was coming off the dock.

"Hey, where have you been?" he asked, since Sally was usually there waiting for him.

"Out where you were." Sally beamed. "It was really something."

"Well, help me with these buckets," her dad answered, "and then I want to hear all about it."

And Sally did.